Chapter 1

WRITTEN BY: JAMES CLARK

INTRODUCTION:

Setting: The gritty streets of Luther St., a neighborhood plagued by drugs, violence, and crime.

- Main Characters:

- Slim: A seasoned pimp who has seen it all but dreams of leaving the game behind.

- Diamond: One of Slim's most trusted hoes, who has her own dreams and secrets.

- Big Mike: A ruthless rival pimp who will stop at nothing to control the streets.

- Grandma Rose: Slim's wise and loving grandmother, who offers him guidance and hope.

TABLE OF CONTENT

EPILOGUE: THE HARSH TRUTH 30

CHAPTER 1: THE GAME BEGINS

The sun dipped below the horizon, casting long shadows over Luther St. The streetlights flickered to life, illuminating the gritty pavement and the faces of those who called this place home. Among them was Slim, a man whose presence commanded respect and fear in equal measure.

Slim leaned against his sleek black car, surveying the scene. His sharp eyes missed nothing—the deals going down in dark alleys, the desperate glances of those looking for their next fix, and the wary looks from those who knew better than to cross him. He was a king in his own right, but the crown weighed heavy on his head.

Diamond approached, her heels clicking against the pavement. She was one of Slim's best, a woman who knew how to play the game and play it well. Her beauty was a weapon, and she wielded it with precision. But tonight, there was something different in her eyes—a flicker of something Slim couldn't quite place.

"Hey, Slim," she greeted, her voice smooth and confident. "Got a minute?"

Slim nodded, motioning for her to join him. "What's on your mind, Diamond?"

She hesitated, glancing around before speaking. "I've been thinking... about getting out. This life, it ain't for me anymore."

Slim's expression hardened. "You know it ain't that simple. The game don't let you go that easy."

Diamond sighed, her shoulders slumping. "I know, but I can't keep doing this. I want something more, something real."

Slim looked at her, seeing the determination in her eyes. He understood her desire to escape, but he also knew the dangers that came with it. "We'll talk more later. For now, keep your head down and stay sharp."

As Diamond walked away, Slim's thoughts drifted to his own dreams of leaving the game. He had seen too much and done too much, and the weight of it all was starting to crush him. But for now, he had to keep playing the role of the king of Luther St.

The night wore on, and Slim continued his rounds, making sure everything was running smoothly. He knew that in this world, trust was a rare commodity, and betrayal lurked around every corner. But he also knew that if he wanted to survive, he had to stay one step ahead of everyone else.

Diamond's Backstory:

Diamond, whose real name is Danielle Johnson, grew up in a small town far from the chaos of Luther St. Her early years were marked by a loving family and a sense of stability. However, everything changed when her father lost his job and turned to alcohol to cope. The once warm and nurturing home became a place of tension and fear.

At 16, Danielle ran away from home, seeking refuge in the city. She quickly learned that the streets were unforgiving. With no money and nowhere to go, she fell in with a rough crowd. It was during this time that she met Big Mike, a charismatic but dangerous man who promised her protection and a way to survive.

Big Mike introduced Danielle to the world of prostitution, giving her the name Diamond for her striking beauty. Under his control, she learned the harsh realities of the game. Despite the dangers, Diamond's resilience and intelligence helped her navigate this new life. She became one of Big Mike's top earners, but the cost was high—her freedom and sense of self were slowly eroded.

Everything changed when she met Slim. Unlike Big Mike, Slim treated her with a level of respect and understanding she hadn't experienced in years. He saw her potential beyond the streets and offered her a chance to work for him. Diamond seized the opportunity, hoping it would be a step towards a better life.

Working for Slim was different. He was tough but fair, and he valued loyalty above all else. Diamond thrived under his guidance, becoming not just a top earner but also a trusted confidante. However, the dream of a better life never left her mind. She saved money secretly, planning for the day she could leave the streets behind for good.

Diamond's relationship with Slim grew complex. She admired him and was grateful for the opportunities he provided, but she also knew that as long as she stayed in the game, true freedom was out of reach. Her desire to escape was fueled by memories of her past and the hope of a future where she could reclaim her identity as Danielle Johnson.

CHAPTER 2: RULES OF THE GAME

The neon lights of Luther St. cast an eerie glow on the pavement as Slim walked the block, his mind racing with thoughts of Diamond's plea to leave the life. He knew the game inside out, every rule, every trick, every betrayal. It was a world where only the sharpest survived, and Slim had honed his instincts to a razor's edge.

Slim's phone buzzed, pulling him from his thoughts. It was a message from one of his girls, Tasha, needing backup at a nearby club. He sighed, knowing that part of his role was to keep his girls safe, even if it meant stepping into dangerous situations.

As he made his way to the club, Slim's mind drifted to the rules that had kept him alive and in control for so long. These were the rules he had learned the hard way and the ones he now passed on to his girls.

- Rule 1: Trust No One. In the game, trust was a luxury no one could afford. Slim had seen too many falls because they trusted the wrong person. He kept his circle tight and his secrets closer. Even Diamond, as much as he cared for her, was not privy to all his plans.
- Rule 2: Loyalty is everything. Loyalty is the currency of the streets. Slim demanded it from his girls and gave it in return. Betrayal was met with swift and unforgiving consequences. It was a harsh reality but one that kept his operation running smoothly.
- Rule 3: Always Stay One Step Ahead The game was constantly changing, and those who couldn't adapt were left behind. Slim prided himself on his ability to anticipate moves before they happened. Whether it was a rival pimp making a play for his territory or a girl thinking about running, Slim was always prepared.
- Rule 4: Protect Your Own Slim's girls were his responsibility. He made sure they were safe, well-

dressed, and knew how to handle themselves. In return, they brought in the money and kept the business thriving. It was a symbiotic relationship built on mutual need and respect.
- Rule 5: Never Show Weakness In a world where strength is everything, showing weakness is a death sentence. Slim kept his emotions in check, his face a mask of calm and control. Even when the pressure mounted, he never let it show.

Slim arrived at the club, his presence immediately commanding attention. Tasha was waiting outside, her eyes wide with fear. "Slim, it's Big Mike's crew. They're inside causing trouble."

Slim nodded, his mind already calculating the best course of action. "Stay here. I'll handle it."

As he stepped into the club, the rules of the game played over in his mind. Trust no one. Loyalty is everything. Always stay one step ahead. Protect your own. Never show weakness. These rules had kept him alive this long, and he wasn't about to break them now.

The club was a cacophony of music and voices, but Slim's focus was on the group of men at the bar. Big Mike's crew. They were loud, aggressive, and clearly looking for trouble. Slim approached, his demeanor calm but his eyes cold.

"Evening, gentlemen," he said, his voice carrying just enough authority to make them pause. "I think it's time you moved along."

One of the men, a hulking figure with a scar across his cheek, sneered. "And who are you to tell us what to do?"

Slim's smile was thin and dangerous. "I'm the one who runs this block. Now, you can leave peacefully, or we can do this the hard way."

The tension in the air was palpable, but Slim didn't waver. He knew the rules, and he knew how to enforce them. The men exchanged glances, weighing their options. Finally, the leader shrugged and motioned for his crew to follow him out.

As they left, Slim felt a surge of relief. Another crisis averted, and another night survived. But he knew it was only a matter of time before the next challenge arose. The game never stopped, and neither could he.

Luther St. Slim's Backstory:

Early Life in Mississippi: Slim was born Jeremiah "Slim" Johnson and grew up in a small, rural town in Mississippi. Life was tough, but his family was close-knit. His mother, Evelyn Johnson, worked multiple jobs to make ends meet, while his older brother, Marcus, took on the role of protector and mentor. Their father had left when Slim was just a baby, leaving Evelyn to raise the boys on her own.

Despite the hardships, Slim's childhood was filled with moments of joy and love. Evelyn instilled in her sons the values of hard work and resilience. Marcus, always the responsible one, dreamed of a better life for his family and often talked about moving north to find better opportunities.

The Move to Pontiac, MI: When Slim was 14, tragedy struck. Marcus was involved in a fatal accident, leaving Evelyn and Slim devastated. The loss of Marcus was a turning point for the family. Evelyn decided it was time to leave Mississippi and start fresh somewhere new. She chose Pontiac, Michigan, hoping the city would offer more opportunities and a chance to escape the painful memories.

The move was challenging. They arrived in Pontiac with little more than the clothes on their backs and a few cherished possessions. Evelyn found work as a nurse's aide, while Slim struggled to adjust to the new environment. The city was a far cry from the rural life he had known, and the streets of Pontiac were filled with dangers and temptations.

Life in Pontiac: In Pontiac, Slim quickly learned that survival required a different set of skills. He fell in with a rough crowd, drawn to the allure of fast money and the sense of belonging it offered. Despite Evelyn's efforts to keep him on the right path, Slim was seduced by street life. He started running small hustles, learning the ropes from older, more experienced hustlers.

Slim's natural charisma and street smarts helped him rise quickly in the ranks. By the time he was 18, he had earned a reputation as a savvy and ruthless player. He adopted the name "Slim" as a nod to his lean build and slick demeanor. The streets of Pontiac became his domain, and he navigated them with a mix of cunning and charm.

The Pimp Game: Slim's entry into the pimp game was almost inevitable. He saw it as a way to gain power and control, something he had craved since losing Marcus. He started small, recruiting a few girls and treating them with a mix of respect and fear. His operation grew, and Slim became known as one of the most successful pimps in Pontiac.

Despite his success, Slim always remembered his roots. He often thought of Marcus and the dreams they had shared. His relationship with his mother remained complicated. Evelyn disapproved of his lifestyle but loved her son unconditionally. She continued to hope that one day, Slim would leave the streets behind and find a better path.

Dreams of a Better Life: As Slim's empire grew, so did his desire to escape the life he had built. He saw the toll it took on those around him and felt the weight of his own actions. The memory of Marcus and the values his mother had instilled in him haunted his thoughts. Slim began to dream of a way out, a chance to start over and build a life free from the violence and betrayal of the streets.

CHAPTER 3: BETRAYAL AND DECEIT

The air was thick with tension as Slim walked the streets of Luther St. He could feel the shift in the atmosphere, a sense of unease that had been growing over the past few weeks. Business was still booming, but there were whispers of discontent and rumors of betrayal. Slim knew better than to ignore such signs.

Diamond had been acting strange lately, more distant and secretive. Slim couldn't shake the feeling that something was off. He had always trusted her, but trust was a fragile thing in their world. He decided it was time to confront her and get to the bottom of whatever was going on.

Slim found Diamond at her usual spot, leaning against a lamppost, her eyes scanning the street. She looked up as he approached, her expression guarded.

"We need to talk," Slim said, his voice low and serious.

Diamond nodded, following him to a quieter spot away from prying eyes and ears. "What's up, Slim?"

"I've been hearing things," Slim began, watching her closely. "Rumors about you planning to leave, maybe even working with Big Mike."

Diamond's eyes widened in shock, but Slim couldn't tell if it was genuine or an act. "Slim, you know I'd never do that. Big Mike? He's the enemy."

Slim sighed, running a hand over his face. "I want to believe you, Diamond, but I need to know the truth. Are you planning to leave?"

Diamond hesitated, then nodded slowly. "Yes, Slim. I want out. But I swear, I'm not working with Big Mike. I just want a better life."

Slim's heart sank. He had known this day would come, but it didn't make it any easier. "Why didn't you come to me? We could have figured something out."

"I didn't think you'd understand," Diamond admitted. "This life… it's killing me, Slim. I need to get out before it's too late."

Before Slim could respond, his phone buzzed. It was a message from one of his boys, Reggie. "Big Mike's making a move. He's hitting our stash house."

Slim's blood ran cold. "Stay here," he ordered Diamond. "I'll deal with this."

He raced to the stash house, his mind racing. If Big Mike was making a move, it meant he had inside information. Someone close to Slim had betrayed him. As he arrived, he saw the aftermath of the attack—broken windows, scattered drugs, and blood on the pavement.

Reggie was waiting for him, a grim look on his face. "We got hit hard, Slim. They knew exactly where to strike."

Slim clenched his fists, anger boiling inside him. "Who was on watch?" "Tasha," Reggie replied. "But she's gone. No sign of her."

Slim's mind raced. Tasha had been loyal, or so he thought. But in this game, loyalty was often a mask for deceit. He needed to find her and get answers.

As Slim and Reggie searched the area, they found Tasha hiding in a nearby alley, her face bruised and scared. "Slim, I didn't mean for this to happen," she pleaded. "Big Mike threatened me. He said he'd kill me if I didn't help him."

Slim's anger softened slightly, but the betrayal still stung. "You should have come to me, Tasha. We could have protected you."

"I'm sorry, Slim," Tasha sobbed. "I was scared."

Slim sighed, knowing that fear was a powerful motivator. "We'll deal with Big Mike, but you need to stay out of sight. This isn't over."

As Slim walked away, his mind was a whirlwind of thoughts. The game was getting more dangerous, and the lines between friend and foe were blurring. He knew he had to stay sharp and trust his instincts. Betrayal and deceit were part of the game, but Slim was determined to come out on top.

Slim's mind was a whirlwind as he considered his next move. Retaliation had to be swift and decisive but also calculated. He couldn't afford to act on impulse; he needed a plan that would send a clear message to Big Mike and anyone else thinking of crossing him.

Step 1: Gather Intelligence Slim knew that information was power. He needed to understand Big Mike's operations, his weaknesses, and his next moves. Slim called a meeting with his most trusted lieutenants, including Reggie and a few others who had proven their loyalty over the years.

"First things first," Slim said, his voice steady. "We need to know everything about Big Mike's setup. Where he's vulnerable, who his key players are, and what his next move might be."

Reggie nodded. "I got a guy on the inside. He can get us the intel we need."

Step 2: Secure the Territory. Slim couldn't afford to lose any more ground. He ordered his crew to tighten security around their key locations. More eyes on the streets, more muscle at the stash houses. He also reached out to a few allies in the neighborhood, ensuring they were on alert and ready to back him up if things got heated.

Step 3: Send a Message Slim needed to make an example out of someone to show that betrayal wouldn't be tolerated. He decided to target one of Big Mike's lower-level enforcers, someone who could be easily reached but whose disappearance would still send shockwaves through Big Mike's crew.

"Reggie, I want you to find Tony, one of Big Mike's boys. Make sure he understands the consequences of crossing us," Slim instructed.

Step 4: Plan the Takeover With the intelligence gathered and his territory secured, Slim began planning a strategic strike against Big Mike. He aimed to hit Big Mike where it hurt the most—his main stash house. Slim knew that taking out Big Mike's primary source of income would cripple his operations and force him into a vulnerable position.

"We'll hit the stash house at dawn," Slim said, outlining the plan. "Reggie, you'll lead the first team. I'll be with the second team, covering the exits. We go in fast and hard, no mistakes."

Step 5: Execute the Plan The night before the raid, Slim gathered his crew for a final briefing. "Remember, this isn't just about taking down Big Mike. It's about sending a message to everyone on Luther St. that we don't tolerate betrayal. Stay sharp, stay focused, and watch each other's backs."

As dawn broke, Slim and his crew moved into position. The raid was swift and brutal, catching Big Mike's men off guard. Within minutes, they had secured the stash house and confiscated drugs and money. Big Mike's operation was in shambles, and the message was clear: Slim was not to be messed with.

Aftermath: With Big Mike's power diminished, Slim solidified his control over Luther St. But he knew the game was far from over.

There would always be new threats, new betrayals. For now, though, he had sent a powerful message and regained the upper hand.

Diamond's Reaction:

Diamond had been on edge ever since Slim left to deal with Big Mike's attack. She knew the stakes were high and that Slim's retaliation would be swift and brutal. As she waited for news, her mind raced with conflicting emotions—fear, guilt, and a glimmer of hope that this might be the turning point for both of them.

When Slim finally returned, his face was a mask of determination and exhaustion. He had taken down Big Mike's stash house, sending a clear message to anyone who dared to betray him. Diamond could see the toll it had taken on him, but there was also a sense of grim satisfaction in his eyes.

"Slim, are you okay?" she asked, her voice trembling slightly.

Slim nodded, his expression softening as he looked at her. "Yeah, we handled it. Big Mike's operation is crippled. But this isn't over, Diamond. We need to stay vigilant."

Diamond felt a surge of relief, but her own guilt quickly overshadowed it. She had been planning to leave, and now, more than ever, she felt trapped between her desire for freedom and her loyalty to Slim.

"I know you did what you had to do," she said, her voice barely above a whisper. "But this life... it's tearing us apart."

Slim sighed, running a hand through his hair. "I know, Diamond. I know. But right now, we need to stick together. We can't afford any more betrayals."

Diamond nodded, understanding the gravity of the situation. She wanted to believe that they could find a way out, that they could escape the violence and deceit that defined their lives. But for now, all she could do was stand by Slim and hope that their loyalty to each other would be enough to see them through.

As the days passed, Diamond watched Slim closely. She saw the weight of his decisions, the burden of leadership that he carried. She knew that his retaliation against Big Mike had been necessary, but it also made her realize just how dangerous their world had become.

In quiet moments, Diamond would dream of a different life—a life where she and Slim could be free from the constant threat of violence and betrayal. She knew it was a long shot, but it was a dream that kept her going, even in the darkest times.

For now, Diamond resolved to stay by Slim's side, to support him as he navigated the treacherous waters of the game. She hoped that one day, they would find a way out together. But until then, she would play her part, knowing that in this world, loyalty was the only thing that could keep them alive.

Slim's Trust in Diamond Wavers:

After the betrayal and the subsequent retaliation against Big Mike, Slim found himself in a state of constant vigilance. The game had always been dangerous, but now it felt like the ground beneath him was shifting. Trust, already a rare commodity, became even more elusive.

Internal Conflict: Slim couldn't shake the nagging doubt that had taken root in his mind. Diamond had been planning to leave, and while she swore she wasn't working with Big Mike, the timing of everything made him question her loyalty. He wanted to believe her, but the game had taught him that trust could be a fatal weakness.

Observing Diamond: Slim began to watch Diamond more closely, looking for any signs of deceit. He noticed the way she interacted with the other girls, the way she seemed more guarded around him. Every small action, every hesitant word, fed into his growing paranoia. He hated feeling this way about someone he cared for, but he couldn't afford to be blindsided again.

Confrontation: One evening, Slim decided to confront Diamond directly. They were alone in his apartment, the tension between them palpable.

"Diamond, I need to know the truth," Slim said, his voice steady but filled with underlying tension. "Were you planning to leave because of Big Mike? Did he get to you?"

Diamond's eyes widened, hurt flashing across her face. "Slim, I told you, I wasn't working with him. I just wanted out. This life… it's too much."

Slim studied her, searching for any hint of a lie. "I want to believe you, Diamond. But after what happened, it's hard to trust anyone."

Diamond stepped closer, her voice soft but firm. "I understand, Slim. But you have to know, I would never betray you. I care about you too much."

Rebuilding Trust: Despite her reassurances, Slim couldn't fully shake his doubts. He decided to keep Diamond close, hoping that time would reveal the truth. He involved her more in his plans, testing her loyalty in subtle ways. He watched how she handled herself and responded to pressure.

Over time, Diamond's actions began to speak louder than words. She proved her loyalty through her dedication and support, standing by Slim even when things got tough. Slowly, Slim's trust in her started to rebuild, but it was a fragile thing, easily shattered by the harsh realities of their world.

A New Understanding: Slim and Diamond's relationship evolved into a complex dance of trust and suspicion. They both knew that in the game, nothing was ever certain. But they also knew that they needed each other to survive. Slim's trust in Diamond wavered, but it never completely broke. It was a testament to the bond they shared, forged in the fires of betrayal and deceit.

Unexpected Twist:

Just as Slim and Diamond begin to rebuild their trust, an unexpected twist threatens to tear them apart once more.

Introduction of a New Player: A new player enters the scene—Rico, a cunning and ambitious young hustler looking to make a name for himself. Rico is smart, ruthless, and has a knack for exploiting weaknesses. He sees an opportunity to rise by taking down Slim and seizing control of Luther St.

Rico's Plan: Rico starts by gathering information on Slim's operation and learning about his key players and their vulnerabilities. He discovers Diamond's past desire to leave the game and decides

to use it against her. Rico approaches Diamond, pretending to be an ally who wants to help her escape. He offers her a way out, but his true intention is to sow discord between her and Slim.

Diamond's Dilemma: Diamond is torn. She desperately wants to believe that Rico's offer is genuine, but she also knows the dangers of trusting a stranger. She decides to keep her interactions with Rico a secret from Slim, fearing that he might see it as another betrayal. However, her secrecy only fuels Slim's growing paranoia.

Rico's Manipulation: Rico continues to manipulate the situation, feeding Slim false information about Diamond's loyalty. He plants seeds of doubt, making Slim question whether Diamond is truly on his side. Rico plans to create a rift between them, weakening Slim's control and making it easier for him to take over.

The Breaking Point: The tension reaches a breaking point when Slim confronts Diamond about her secret meetings with Rico. Diamond tries to explain, but Slim's trust is shattered once again. He feels betrayed and lashes out, accusing her of conspiring against him. Diamond, hurt and frustrated, decides to leave, believing that Slim will never trust her again.

Rico's Move: With Diamond gone and Slim's operation in disarray, Rico makes his move. He launches a coordinated attack on Slim's remaining assets, aiming to take control of Luther St. Slim, now isolated and vulnerable, and realizes that Rico has been playing them all along.

A Desperate Gamble: In a desperate gamble to save his empire and win back Diamond's trust, Slim decides to confront Rico directly. He reaches out to Diamond, explaining the situation and asking for her help. Despite her anger and hurt, Diamond agrees to join forces with Slim one last time.

The Final Showdown: Slim and Diamond devise a plan to outsmart Rico and reclaim control of Luther St. The showdown is intense and dangerous, with both sides risking everything. In the end, Slim and Diamond manage to outmaneuver Rico, exposing his treachery and restoring their dominance.

Rebuilding Trust: The ordeal leaves Slim and Diamond scarred but stronger. They realize that their only chance of surviving the game is by trusting each other completely. Together, they begin to rebuild their operation, vowing to never let anyone come between them again.

Rico's Role in the Neighborhood:

Rico is a rising figure in the neighborhood, known for his ambition and ruthlessness. Unlike the established players like Slim and Big Mike, Rico is relatively new to the scene but has quickly made a name for himself through his cunning and strategic thinking.

Key Aspects of Rico's Role:

- **Ambitious Hustler:** Rico is driven by a desire to climb the ranks and establish his own empire. He sees the chaos and power struggles in the neighborhood as opportunities to exploit and gain control. His ambition makes him a dangerous adversary, as he is willing to take significant risks to achieve his goals.
- **Manipulator:** Rico excels at manipulation, using his charm and intelligence to turn people against each other. He identifies weaknesses and exploits them, creating rifts and sowing discord among his rivals. His ability to manipulate situations and people makes him a formidable opponent.
- **Information Broker:** Rico understands the value of information and has built a network of informants and spies. He gathers intelligence on his rivals, learning their secrets and vulnerabilities. This knowledge allows him to stay one step ahead and plan his moves with precision.
- **Strategic Planner:** Unlike some of the more impulsive players in the neighborhood, Rico is a strategic thinker. He carefully plans his actions, considering the long-term consequences and potential benefits. His calculated approach makes him a significant threat to anyone who underestimates him.

- **Disruptor:** Rico's presence in the neighborhood disrupts the existing power dynamics. He challenges the established order, creating instability and forcing other players to adapt. His actions often lead to increased tension and conflict as he seeks to destabilize his rivals and seize control.
- **Charismatic Leader:** Despite his ruthless nature, Rico has a certain charisma that attracts followers. He knows how to inspire loyalty and motivate his crew, promising them power and wealth. His ability to rally people to his cause makes him a dangerous and influential figure in the neighborhood.

Impact on the Neighborhood: Rico's rise to power brings a new level of danger and unpredictability to the neighborhood. His strategic mind and manipulative tactics create an environment of constant tension and mistrust. As he continues to challenge the established players, the neighborhood becomes a battleground for control and survival.

Rico's role as a disruptor and manipulator forces Slim and others to stay vigilant and adapt to the changing landscape. His presence ensures that the game remains treacherous, with alliances shifting and betrayals lurking around every corner.

Tense Confrontation Between Slim and Rico:

The alley was dimly lit, shadows dancing on the walls as the flickering streetlight struggled to pierce the darkness. The air was thick with the smell of garbage and the distant hum of the city. Slim stood at one end, his silhouette sharp against the faint glow. He was waiting, his eyes scanning the alley for any sign of movement.

Rico emerged from the shadows, his steps confident and deliberate. He wore a smirk that hinted at his arrogance, a stark contrast to the tension that hung in the air. Slim's jaw tightened as he watched Rico approach, every muscle in his body coiled and ready for whatever might come next.

"Evening, Slim," Rico greeted, his voice smooth and mocking. "Didn't think you'd show up alone."

Slim's eyes narrowed. "I don't need backup to deal with you, Rico. You think you're smart, playing your little games. But you made a mistake coming after me."

Rico chuckled, the sound echoing off the brick walls. "Mistake? Nah, Slim. I'm just getting started. You see, this neighborhood needs a new king, and I'm here to take the throne."

Slim took a step forward, his presence imposing. "You think you can just waltz in and take what's mine? You don't know the first thing about running these streets."

Rico's smirk faded, replaced by a cold, calculating look. "I know enough to see that you're slipping. Your own people are turning on you. Diamond, Tasha… they're just the beginning."

Slim's fists clenched at the mention of Diamond. "Leave them out of this. This is between you and me."

Rico shrugged, his eyes gleaming with malice. "Oh, but they are part of this, Slim. Everyone is. You can't trust anyone in this game. Not even your precious Diamond."

The words hit Slim like a punch to the gut, but he didn't let it show. He took another step forward, closing the distance between them. "You talk a big game, Rico. But talk is cheap. You want to take me down? You'll have to do it yourself."

Rico's hand moved to his waistband, where a glint of metal caught the light. Slim's eyes flicked to the gun, but he didn't flinch. He knew this was a test, a moment that would define their rivalry.

"Careful, Slim," Rico warned, his voice low and dangerous. "You don't want to make a move you'll regret."

Slim's gaze was steady, unwavering. "The only regret here will be yours, Rico. You think you can scare me? I've been through worse than you can imagine."

For a moment, the alley was silent, the tension between them crackling like electricity. Then, with a sudden movement, Slim lunged forward, his hand striking out to knock the gun from Rico's grip. The weapon clattered to the ground, and the two men were locked in a fierce struggle.

Slim's strength and experience gave him the upper hand, but Rico's desperation made him a formidable opponent. They grappled in the dim light, each trying to gain the upper hand. Finally, Slim managed to pin Rico against the wall, his forearm pressing against Rico's throat.

"This is your last chance," Slim hissed, his voice filled with menace. "Leave Luther St. and never come back. If I see you again, I won't be so merciful."

Rico's eyes burned with hatred, but he nodded, knowing he was beaten. Slim released him, stepping back and watching as Rico stumbled away, clutching his throat.

As Rico disappeared into the shadows, Slim stood alone in the alley, his heart pounding. He knew this was far from over, but for now, he had sent a clear message. The game was still his, and he would do whatever it took to keep it that way.

Rico has managed to uncover several secrets about Slim that he plans to use to his advantage:

- **Slim's Past in Mississippi:** Rico knows about Slim's early life in Mississippi, including the tragic loss of his brother Marcus and the move to Pontiac, MI. He understands the emotional scars this has left on Slim and sees it as a potential vulnerability.
- **Slim's Relationship with Diamond:** Rico is aware of Slim's complex and often strained relationship with Diamond. He knows about Diamond's past desire to leave the game and her secret meetings with him. Rico plans to exploit this tension to drive a wedge between them.
- **Slim's Financial Struggles:** Despite his outward success, Slim has been facing financial difficulties. Rico has discovered that Slim's operation is not as stable as it appears, with debts and cash flow issues threatening to undermine his control. Rico intends to use this information to further destabilize Slim's empire.
- **Connections to Law Enforcement**: Rico has learned that Slim has a few contacts within the local police force, individuals who have been turning a blind eye to his activities in exchange for bribes. Rico plans to expose these connections, potentially bringing legal trouble to Slim and weakening his position.
- **Slim's Plans to Leave the Game:** Rico has caught wind of Slim's secret desire to leave the pimp game and start anew. He knows that Slim has been quietly making plans to exit life, and he intends to use this knowledge to create doubt and mistrust among Slim's crew, making them question his commitment and loyalty.
- **Personal Weaknesses:** Rico has observed Slim's personal habits and weaknesses, such as his occasional reliance on alcohol to cope with stress. Rico sees these as opportunities to exploit, potentially setting traps that could lead Slim into compromising situations.

By leveraging these secrets, Rico aims to undermine Slim's authority and take control of Luther St. He knows that exposing these vulnerabilities at the right moment could bring Slim's carefully constructed world to a crashing halt.

CHAPTER 4: STANDING ON BUSINESS

The night was eerily quiet as Slim made his way through the back alleys of Luther St. The weight of his decision pressed heavily on his shoulders, but he knew there was no turning back. Rico had pushed him too far, and now it was time to end this once and for all.

Slim had spent the past few days gathering intel, planning every detail of his move. He knew Rico's routines, his hideouts, and his weaknesses. Tonight, Rico was holed up in an abandoned warehouse on the outskirts of the neighborhood, surrounded by a few loyal but expendable men.

As Slim approached the warehouse, he signaled to Reggie and the rest of his crew to take their positions. They moved silently, like shadows in the night, ready to strike at a moment's notice. Slim took a deep breath, steeling himself for what was to come.

Inside the warehouse, Rico was lounging in a makeshift office, a smug grin on his face as he counted a stack of cash. He had no idea that his time was running out. Slim stepped into the room, his presence immediately commanding attention.

"Rico," Slim said, his voice cold and steady. "It's over."

Rico looked up, surprise flickering across his face before it was replaced by a sneer. "Slim. I was wondering when you'd show up. Come to beg for mercy?"

Slim shook his head, his eyes locked on Rico. "No. I've come to end this."

Rico's hand moved towards his waistband, but Slim was faster. In a flash, he drew his gun, aiming it squarely at Rico's chest. "Don't even think about it."

The room was tense, the air thick with anticipation. Rico's men, sensing the danger, began to move, but Reggie and Slim's crew were already in position, guns drawn and ready.

"You're making a big mistake, Slim," Rico said, his voice dripping with arrogance. "You kill me, and you'll never be able to trust anyone again."

Slim's grip tightened on the gun. "I already can't trust anyone. But I can make sure you don't hurt anyone else."

Rico's eyes narrowed, realizing that Slim was serious. "You think this will solve anything? The game will go on, with or without me."

Slim took a step closer, his resolve unshaken. "Maybe. But it won't go on with you."

With a final, decisive movement, Slim pulled the trigger. The gunshot echoed through the warehouse, and Rico fell to the ground, his eyes wide with shock. The room fell silent, the only sound the faint ringing in Slim's ears.

Slim lowered his gun, his heart pounding. He had done what needed to be done, but the weight of his actions settled heavily on him. He turned to Reggie and the crew, who were watching him with a mix of respect and apprehension.

"Clean this up," Slim ordered, his voice steady. "And make sure everyone knows—this is what happens to those who betray us."

As Slim walked out of the warehouse, the night air felt colder, sharper. He knew that the game would never truly be over, but for now, he had reclaimed control. He had sent a message that would echo through the streets of Luther St., a message that betrayal would not be tolerated.

CHAPTER 5: THE FINAL SHOWDOWN

The tension in the air was palpable as Slim prepared for the final confrontation with Big Mike. The stakes had never been higher, and Slim knew that this battle would determine the future of Luther St. He had spent weeks planning, gathered intel, and rallied his crew. Now, it was time to put everything on the line.

Setting the Stage: The showdown was set to take place in an abandoned warehouse on the outskirts of the neighborhood. It was a fitting location—dark, isolated, and filled with echoes of past conflicts. Slim's crew was positioned strategically around the perimeter, ready to strike at a moment's notice. Reggie stood by Slim's side; his loyalty unwavering.

As Slim approached the warehouse, he could see Big Mike's men milling about, their faces stern and ready for a fight. Big Mike himself stood at the entrance, a menacing figure with a cold, calculating gaze. Slim took a deep breath, steeling himself for what was to come.

The Confrontation: Slim and Big Mike locked eyes, the animosity between them crackling like electricity. Slim stepped forward, his voice steady and commanding. "This ends tonight, Mike. No more games, no more betrayals. Just you and me."

Big Mike's lips curled into a sneer. "You think you can take me down, Slim? I've been running these streets long before you showed up. You're just a pretender."

Slim's jaw tightened, but he kept his composure. "We'll see about that."

With a signal from Big Mike, his men moved to surround Slim and his crew. The tension was thick, every muscle in Slim's body coiled and ready to spring into action. He knew that this would be a fight to the death, and he was prepared to do whatever it took to come out on top.

The Battle: The first shots rang out, shattering the silence of the night. Slim and his crew moved with precision, their training and experience evident in every calculated move. The warehouse erupted into chaos, the sound of gunfire and shouts echoing off the walls.

Slim focused on Big Mike, weaving through the melee with a single-minded determination. He dodged bullets and returned fire, his eyes never leaving his target. Big Mike was a formidable opponent, but Slim's resolve was unbreakable.

As the battle raged on, Slim finally closed the distance between them. The two men faced off, their guns drawn and ready. For a moment, time seemed to stand still, the world narrowing down to just the two of them.

The Final Duel: Big Mike lunged forward, his gun aimed at Slim's chest. Slim reacted instinctively, sidestepping the attack and delivering a powerful blow to Big Mike's jaw. The gun clattered to the ground, and the two men grappled in a brutal hand-to-hand fight.

Slim's strength and agility gave him the upper hand, but Big Mike's sheer size and brutality made him a dangerous adversary. They traded blows, each one more vicious than the last. Slim could feel the exhaustion setting in, but he pushed through, fueled by the need to protect his crew and his territory.

With a final, desperate surge of energy, Slim managed to disarm Big Mike and pin him to the ground. He pressed his gun to Big Mike's temple, his voice low and filled with resolve. "It's over, Mike. This is for everyone you've hurt."

Big Mike's eyes flashed with defiance, but he knew he was beaten. "Do it, then. End it."

Slim hesitated for a moment, the weight of his decision pressing down on him. But he knew there was no other way. With a steady hand, he pulled the trigger, ending Big Mike's reign of terror once and for all.

Aftermath: The warehouse fell silent, the echoes of the battle fading into the night. Slim stood over Big Mike's lifeless body, his heart pounding. He had won, but the cost had been high. He turned to his crew, who were already tending to the wounded and securing the area.

Reggie approached his face, a mix of relief and respect. "We did it, Slim. Luther St. is ours."

Slim nodded, his mind already racing with thoughts of what came next. He knew that the game would never truly be over, but for now, they had secured their place. He looked around at his crew, the people who had stood by him through thick and thin, and felt a surge of gratitude.

As they left the warehouse, Slim knew that the road ahead would be filled with challenges. But with his crew by his side and the memory of those they had lost driving him forward, he was ready to face whatever came next.

Diamond's Reaction:

Diamond was in her small apartment, trying to find a moment of peace amidst the chaos that had engulfed their lives. The news of the showdown between Slim and Big Mike had spread quickly, but she hadn't heard the outcome yet. Her heart was heavy with worry, knowing that Slim was risking everything.

When the knock on her door came, she jumped, her nerves frayed. She opened it to find Reggie standing there, his expression serious but with a hint of relief.

"Reggie, what happened?" she asked, her voice trembling.

"It's over, Diamond," Reggie said, stepping inside. "Big Mike is dead. Slim took him down."

Diamond's breath caught in her throat. She felt a rush of conflicting emotions—relief that Slim was safe but also a deep sense of unease. She had known Big Mike for years, and despite everything, his death marked the end of an era.

"Is Slim okay?" she asked, her voice barely above a whisper.

Reggie nodded. "He's fine. A little banged up, but he'll be alright. He wanted me to check on you, make sure you're safe."

Diamond sank onto the couch, her mind racing. She had always known that the game was dangerous, but the reality of it was hitting her hard. Big Mike's death was a stark reminder of the life they were living and the constant threat that hung over them.

"Thank you, Reggie," she said, her voice steadying. "I need to see Slim." Reggie nodded. "He's at the warehouse, cleaning up. I'll take you there."

As they made their way to the warehouse, Diamond's thoughts were a whirlwind. She knew that Slim had done what he had to do, but the violence and danger of their world were becoming more

challenging to bear. She had always dreamed of a way out, and now, more than ever, she felt the urgency of that dream.

When they arrived at the warehouse, Diamond saw Slim standing amidst the aftermath of the battle. He looked tired, but she recognized the determination in his eyes. He turned as she approached, his expression softening.

"Diamond," he said, his voice filled with relief. "I'm glad you're here."

She rushed to him, wrapping her arms around him in a tight embrace. "Slim, I was so worried. I'm glad you're okay."

Slim held her close, feeling the weight of the past few days lift slightly. "It's over, Diamond. Big Mike is gone. But we need to stay strong. There's still a lot to do."

Diamond pulled back, looking into his eyes. "I know, Slim. But we can't keep living like this. We need to find a way out, for both of us."

Slim nodded, understanding the truth in her words. "We'll find a way, Diamond. I promise. But for now, we need to stick together and rebuild."

As they stood there, surrounded by the remnants of the battle, Diamond felt a renewed sense of hope. She knew that the road ahead would be difficult, but with Slim by her side, she believed they could find a way to escape the life that had trapped them for so long.

CHAPTER 6: THE NEW BEGINNING

The sun rose over Luther St., casting a warm glow on the neighborhood that had seen so much turmoil. For the first time in a long while, there was a sense of calm in the air. Slim stood on the steps of his apartment, looking out at the street that had been both his kingdom and his prison.

Rebuilding Trust: Slim knew that the road ahead would be challenging, but he was determined to make a fresh start. He had spent the past few weeks rebuilding his operation, ensuring that his crew was loyal and that his territory was secure. The death of Big Mike had sent a clear message, but it also left a power vacuum that Slim needed to fill carefully.

A New Vision: Slim called a meeting with his most trusted lieutenants, including Reggie and Diamond. They gathered in a small, dimly lit room, the weight of their shared experiences hanging in the air.

"We've been through a lot," Slim began, his voice steady. "But it's time to look forward. We need to build something better, something that can last."

Reggie nodded, his respect for Slim evident. "What do you have in mind, Slim?"

Slim took a deep breath. "We need to diversify. The game is changing, and we need to change with it. I want to invest in legitimate businesses, create opportunities for our people that don't involve violence and crime."

Diamond's eyes lit up with hope. "You mean, we could actually get out of this life?"

Slim nodded. "Yes. It's not going to be easy, but it's possible. We start small, build up our resources, and slowly transition out of the game."

First Steps: Slim and his crew began to put their plan into action. They invested in a local bar, turning it into a legitimate business that provided jobs and a safe space for the community. They also started a small security company, offering protection services to local businesses and residents.

The transition was challenging. There were still threats from rival gangs and the ever-present danger of law enforcement. But Slim's determination and strategic thinking helped them navigate these obstacles.

Strengthening Bonds: As they worked together to build their new ventures, the bonds between Slim, Diamond, and the rest of the crew grew stronger. They faced setbacks and successes together, learning to trust each other in ways they never had before.

Slim and Diamond's relationship deepened, built on a foundation of shared dreams and mutual respect. They supported each other through the tough times, finding solace in their partnership.

A Glimmer of Hope: Months passed, and the neighborhood began to change. The bar became a popular spot, known for its welcoming atmosphere and good music. The security company gained a reputation for reliability and professionalism. Slowly but surely, Slim's vision of a better future started to take shape.

One evening, as the sun set over Luther St., Slim and Diamond stood outside the bar, watching the people come and go. There was a sense of pride and accomplishment in the air, a feeling that they were finally on the right path.

"We did it, Slim," Diamond said, her voice filled with emotion. "We actually did it."

Slim smiled, wrapping an arm around her shoulders. "Yeah, we did. But this is just the beginning. There's still a lot of work to do."

Diamond nodded, her eyes shining with determination. "I know. But for the first time, I feel like we have a real chance."

As they stood there, looking out at the neighborhood they had fought so hard to protect, Slim felt a sense of peace. The game would always be a part of their past, but now they had a future to look forward to—a future built on hope, resilience, and the promise of a new beginning.

CHAPTER 7: THE FINAL SACRIFICE

Thanks to Slim's vision and determination, the neighborhood had begun to change. The bar was thriving, the security company was gaining respect, and there was a sense of hope that hadn't been felt in years. But the game had a way of pulling people back in, and Slim knew that peace was always fragile.

A New Threat: Despite their efforts to go legitimate, there were still those who wanted to see Slim fall. A new gang, led by a ruthless figure named Trey, saw Slim's success as a threat to their own ambitions. They began to encroach on Slim's territory, causing trouble and stirring up old rivalries.

Slim tried to handle it diplomatically, but Trey was not interested in peace. He wanted control, and he was willing to do whatever it took to get it. The tension escalated, and it became clear that a confrontation was inevitable.

The Final Stand: One night, Trey and his crew launched a full-scale attack on the bar, hoping to send a message and take over Slim's operations. Slim and his crew were ready, but the fight was brutal and chaotic. Gunfire echoed through the streets, and the bar that had become a symbol of hope was turned into a battleground.

Slim fought with everything he had, determined to protect what they had built. He moved through the chaos with a fierce determination, his mind focused on one goal: to end the threat once and for all.

The Ultimate Sacrifice: In the midst of the battle, Slim saw Trey aiming a gun at Diamond, who was trying to help the wounded. Without a second thought, Slim threw himself in front of her, taking the bullet meant for her. The pain was immediate and intense, but Slim didn't falter. He managed to disarm Trey and take him down, ensuring that the threat was neutralized.

As the dust settled, Slim collapsed to the ground, his vision blurring. Diamond was by his side in an instant, her hands trembling as she tried to stop the bleeding.

"Slim, stay with me," she pleaded, tears streaming down her face.

Slim looked up at her, his strength fading. "Diamond… you have to keep going. Build a better life… for both of us."

Diamond shook her head, her heart breaking. "No, Slim. You can't leave me. We need you."

Slim managed a weak smile, his hand reaching up to touch her face. "You can do it, Diamond. I believe in you."

With those final words, Slim's eyes closed, and he took his last breath. The neighborhood that had been his kingdom fell silent, the weight of his sacrifice hanging heavy in the air.

Aftermath: Slim's death was a devastating blow, but his legacy lived on. Diamond, Reggie, and the rest of the crew vowed to honor his memory by continuing the work he had started. They rebuilt the bar, expanded the security company, and invested in new ventures that provided opportunities for the community.

Diamond emerged as a strong and determined leader, driven by the promise she had made to Slim. She faced challenges and setbacks, but she never wavered in her commitment to building a better future.

A Lasting Legacy: Years later, the neighborhood had transformed. The streets were safer, the businesses were thriving, and there was a sense of hope that had once seemed impossible. Slim's name became synonymous with resilience and change, a reminder of the man who had given everything to protect his people.

Diamond often visited Slim's grave, a quiet spot overlooking the neighborhood he had loved. She would sit and talk to him, sharing the successes and struggles of their journey. And every time, she would leave with a renewed sense of purpose, knowing that Slim's spirit was with her, guiding her every step of the way.

EPILOGUE: THE HARSH TRUTH

Luther street had changed, but the lessons learned there remained etched in the hearts of those who survived. Slim's sacrifice had brought temporary peace, but the underlying truth of the game was something no one could escape.

Diamond's Reflection: Diamond stood at the edge of the neighborhood, looking out at the bustling streets that had once been a battleground. The businesses were thriving, and there was a sense of community that Slim had always dreamed of. But she knew better than anyone that the peace was fragile.

She had taken up Slim's mantle, leading with strength and determination. Yet, the lessons of the past were never far from her mind. She had learned the hard way that trust was a rare and dangerous commodity. Even those closest to you could turn, and the game had a way of pulling you back in when you least expected it.

A Constant Vigilance: Diamond's eyes scanned the crowd, always alert for signs of trouble. She had built a network of loyal allies, but she never let her guard down. The memory of Slim's final words echoed in her mind, a constant reminder of the harsh realities they faced.

"Never trust no one, and you're never safe."

These words had become her mantra, guiding her actions and decisions. She knew that the game was never truly over and that safety was an illusion. The only way to survive was to stay vigilant and prepared for anything.

A Legacy of Resilience: Despite the constant threat, Diamond found strength in the legacy Slim had left behind. His vision of a better future had given her purpose, and she was determined to honor his memory by continuing the work they had started. She invested in the community, created opportunities for those who wanted to escape life, and built a network of support for those who needed it.

But she always remembered the lessons of the streets. She knew that betrayal could come from anywhere and that trust was a luxury she couldn't afford. The game had taught her to be strong, to be smart, and to always be one step ahead.

A New Generation: As the years passed, a new generation grew up in the neighborhood, unaware of the battles that had been fought to give them a chance at a better life. Diamond watched them with a mix of hope and caution, knowing that the cycle could easily repeat itself.

She made it her mission to educate them and share the hard-earned lessons of the past. She wanted them to understand the dangers and to be prepared for the harsh realities of the world. But she also

wanted them to believe in the possibility of change, to carry forward the dream that Slim had died for.

The Harsh Truth: In the end, Luther St.'s story was a testament to the resilience of the human spirit. It was a story of sacrifice, dreams, and the harsh truths that defined their world. Diamond knew that they could never truly escape the game, but they could learn to navigate it, to survive and thrive despite the odds.

As she stood there, watching the sun set over the neighborhood, Diamond felt a sense of peace. She had learned to live with the uncertainty, to find strength in the struggle. And she knew that as long as she remembered the lessons of the past, she could face whatever the future held.

The End

The story of Luther St. Slim is one of resilience, sacrifice, and the harsh truths of life on the streets. Slim's journey from Mississippi to Pontiac, MI, his rise to power, and his ultimate sacrifice left an indelible mark on the neighborhood and the people he cared about.

Diamond, Reggie, and the rest of the crew carried forward his legacy, always remembering the lessons he taught them: never trust anyone completely, and never assume you're safe. The game was relentless, but so was their determination to build a better future.

In the end, Slim's dream of a better life lived on through those who survived is a testament to his strength and vision. The streets of Luther St. would never forget the man who gave everything to protect his people, and his spirit continued to guide them as they navigated the challenges of their world.

Written by: James Clark

Made in the USA
Coppell, TX
18 November 2024

40448669R00024